187207

PowerKids Readers:

# The Bilingual Library of the
# United States of America™

# ALABAMA

**VANESSA BROWN**

Traducción al español: María Cristina Brusca

The Rosen Publishing Group's
PowerKids Press™ & **Editorial Buenas Letras**™
New York

Published in 2005 by The Rosen Publishing Group, Inc.
29 East 21st Street, New York, NY 10010

First Edition

Photo Credits: Cover © Robert Harding World Imagery/Getty Images; p. 5 © Joe Sohm/ The Image Works; p. 9 © William A. Bake/Corbis; pp. 11, 31 (mound) © Richard A. Cooke; p. 13 © Corbis; pp. 15, 17, 31 (Parks, Wallace, Cole, Lee, Aaron, march) © Bettmann/Corbis; p. 19 © Charles E. Rotkin/Corbis;  p. 21 © Nathan Benn/Corbis; p. 23 © JLP/Sylvia Torres/Corbis; pp. 25, 30 (capital) © Joseph Sohm; ChromoSohm Inc./Corbis; pp. 26, 30 (tree) © Lightwave Photography, Inc./Animals Animals/Earth Scenes; p. 30 (bird) © Roger Wilmhurst; Frank Lane Picture Agency/Corbis; p. 30 (flower) © Peter Smithers/Corbis; p. 30 (quartz) © Richard Kolar/Animals Animals/Earth Scenes; p. 31 (Owens) © Hulton-Deutsch Collection/Corbis; p. 31 (waterfall) © Digital Vision

Library of Congress Cataloging-in-Publication Data

Brown, Vanessa, 1963-
  Alabama / Vanessa Brown ; traducción al español, María Cristina Brusca.– 1st ed.
      p. cm. – (The bilingual library of the United States of America)
  Includes bibliographical references and index.
  ISBN 1-4042-3065-3 (library binding)
  1.  Alabama–Juvenile literature.  I. Title. II. Series.

  F326.3.B767 2006
  976.1–dc22
                                                    2004029733

Manufactured in the United States of America

Due to the changing nature of Internet links, Editorial Buenas Letras has developed an online list of Web sites related to the subject of this book. This site is updated regularly. Please use this link to access the list:

http://www.buenasletraslinks.com/ls/alabama

# Contents

# Contenido

## Welcome to Alabama

These are the flag and seal of Alabama. The seal has a map of the state and its rivers. The seal shows Alabama's great rivers.

---

## Bienvenidos a Alabama

Éstos son la bandera y el escudo de Alabama. El escudo tiene el mapa del estado. El escudo muestra los grandes ríos de Alabama.

Alabama Flag and State Seal

Bandera y escudo de Alabama

## Alabama Geography

Alabama borders the states of Mississippi, Tennessee, Georgia, and Florida. Alabama also borders the ocean in the Gulf of Mexico.

---

## Geografía de Alabama

Alabama limita con los estados de Misisipi, Tennessee, Georgia y Florida. Alabama también linda con el océano en el golfo de México.

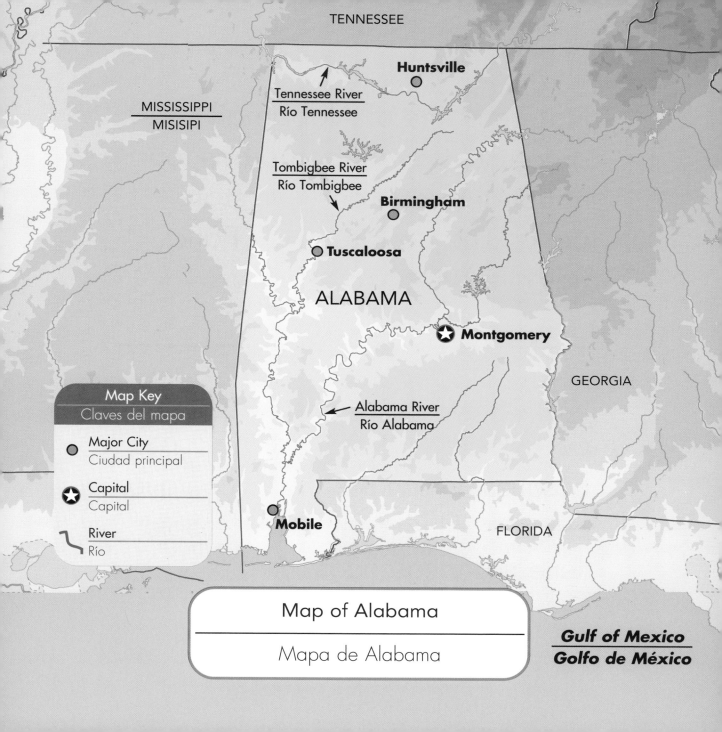

TENNESSEE

MISSISSIPPI
MISISIPI

**Huntsville**

Tennessee River
Río Tennessee

Tombigbee River
Río Tombigbee

**Birmingham**

**Tuscaloosa**

ALABAMA

★ **Montgomery**

GEORGIA

Alabama River
Río Alabama

**Map Key**
Claves del mapa

Major City
Ciudad principal

★ Capital
Capital

River
Río

**Mobile**

FLORIDA

Map of Alabama

Mapa de Alabama

*Gulf of Mexico*
*Golfo de México*

Nature is one of Alabama's greatest gifts. Alabama has four national forests and five state parks. The DeSoto State Park has rivers and waterfalls.

---

La naturaleza es uno de los tesoros de Alabama. Alabama tiene cuatro bosques nacionales y cinco parques estatales. El Parque Estatal DeSoto tiene ríos y cascadas.

Little River Canyon
_____

Cañón del Little River

## Alabama History

People have lived in Alabama for almost 10,000 years! These first Alabamians lived in villages and built mounds.

---

## Historia de Alabama

¡Los seres humanos han vivido en Alabama por casi 10,000 años! Los primeros alabamienses vivían en pueblos y construyeron montículos.

View of Mounds at Moundville Park

Vista de montículos en el Parque Moundville

Alabama took part in the Civil War. The Civil War was fought between the North and the South from 1861 to 1865. An important sea battle was fought in Mobile Bay, Alabama, in 1864.

---

Alabama participó en la Guerra Civil entre el Norte y el Sur. La Guerra Civil duró desde 1861 hasta 1865. Una importante batalla naval tuvo lugar en la Bahía Mobile, en Alabama en 1864.

Battle of Mobile Bay in 1864

Batalla de la Bahía de Mobile en 1864

In 1955, Rosa Parks refused to give up her seat to a white man on a bus. Rosa's refusal was against the law. She was arrested. Her actions marked the beginning of the civil rights movement. This movement gave equal rights to African Americans.

En 1955, Rosa Parks se negó a cederle su asiento en el autobús a un hombre blanco. Esto iba en contra de la ley. Rosa fue arrestada. Sus acciones marcaron el comienzo del movimiento por los derechos civiles. Este movimiento le dio igualdad de derechos a los afroamericanos.

Rosa Parks Riding the Bus

Rosa Parks en el autobús

Martin Luther King Jr. was a leader of the civil rights movement. In 1965, he led an important march in Montgomery, Alabama. This march gave African Americans the right to vote.

---

Martin Luther King Jr. fue un líder del movimiento por los derechos civiles. En 1965, encabezó una importante marcha en Montgomery, Alabama. Gracias a esta marcha los afroamericanos ganaron su derecho a votar.

Martin Luther King Jr. Leads a March in 1965

Martin Luther King Jr. encabeza una marcha en 1965

## Living in Alabama

Birmingham is Alabama's largest city. This city has been producing steel for more than a century. Birmingham is called the Magic City.

---

## La vida en Alabama

Birmingham es la ciudad más grande de Alabama. Esta ciudad ha producido acero durante más de un siglo. Birmingham es conocida como la Ciudad Mágica.

View of the City of Birmingham and Steel Mills

Vista de la ciudad de Birmingham y de las acerías

French settlers brought the festival of Mardi Gras to Mobile, Alabama, in 1703. Mardi Gras marks the beginning of Easter. Easter is a Christian celebration.

---

Los colonos franceses trajeron el festival de *Mardi Gras* a Mobile, Alabama, en 1703. *Mardi Gras* marca el comienzo de la Pascua. La pascua es una fiesta cristiana.

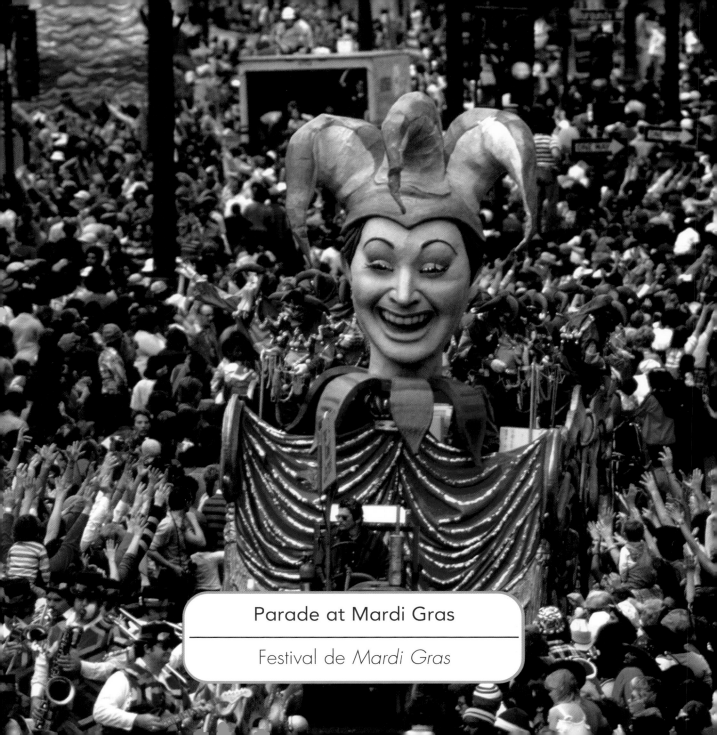

Parade at Mardi Gras

Festival de *Mardi Gras*

## Alabama Today

Alabama is ready for the future. The Alabama Supercomputer Center connects government, business, and schools to the Internet. This supercomputer helps all Alabamians.

---

## Alabama, hoy

Alabama está preparada para el futuro. El Centro de Supercomputadoras de Alabama conecta el gobierno, los negocios y las escuelas a la Internet. Esta supercomputadora ayuda a todos los alabamienses.

Schools in Alabama Are Connected with the Internet

Las escuelas en Alabama están conectadas a la Internet

Birmingham, Mobile, Montgomery, and Huntsville are important cities in Alabama. Montgomery is the capital of the state of Alabama.

---

Birmingham, Mobile, Montgomery y Huntsville son ciudades importantes de Alabama. Montgomery es la capital de Alabama.

Alabama State Capitol in Montgomery

Capitolio de Alabama en Montgomery

# Activity:

## Let´s Draw Alabama's State Tree

The Southern longleaf pine was named Alabama's official state tree in 1997.

---

# Actividad:

## Dibujemos el árbol de Alabama

El piñonero fue nombrado el árbol oficial de Alabama en 1997.

**1**

Draw a tall, thin triangle. This is the trunk.

Dibuja un triángulo alto y delgado. Éste es el tronco.

**2**

For the branches draw lines on either side of the trunk.

Para dibujar las ramas traza líneas a cada lado del tronco.

**3**

Draw crooked lines for the branches.

Traza líneas torcidas para formar más ramas.

**4**

Turn your pencil on its side and shade from side to side on top of the trunk and branches.

Toma tu lápiz de costado y sombrea la parte de arriba del tronco y las ramas.

**5**

To draw the leaves, darken the shaded area and the branches as shown. Great job!

Para dibujar las hojas oscurece el área sombreada y las ramas, como se ve en la muestra. ¡Muy bien!

# Timeline      Cronología

| | | |
|---|---|---|
| Spanish explorer Hernando de Soto explores Alabama. | **1540** | El explorador español Hernando de Soto explora Alabama. |
| Alabama becomes the twenty-second state. | **1819** | Alabama se convierte en el estado número veintidós. |
| Alabama separates from the United States and becomes the Republic of Alabama. | **1861** | Alabama se separa de Estados Unidos y se convierte en la República de Alabama. |
| Alabama rejoins the United States. | **1868** | Alabama se une nuevamente a los Estados Unidos. |
| Rosa Parks refuses to give up her seat on a bus. Her actions mark the beginning of the civil rights movement. | **1955** | Rosa Parks se niega a ceder su asiento en un autobús. Sus acciones marcan el comienzo del movimiento por los derechos civiles. |
| The National Civil Rights Museum opens in Birmingham. | **1991** | El Museo Nacional de los Derechos Civiles se inaugura en Birmingham. |

# Alabama Events

## Eventos en Alabama

| Alabama Events | Eventos en Alabama |
|---|---|
| **February-March**<br>Mardi Gras in Mobile<br>Azalea Spectacular in Mobile | Febrero-marzo<br>Mardi Gras, en Mobile<br>Festival de la azalea, en Mobile |
| **March**<br>Selma Pilgrimage Weekend | Marzo<br>Fin de semana de peregrinación, en Selma |
| **April**<br>Birmingham Festival of Arts | Abril<br>Festival de las Artes de Birmingham |
| **May**<br>Birmingham Rose Show | Mayo<br>Exposición de las rosas de Birmingham |
| **August**<br>River Boat Regatta in Guntersville | Agosto<br>Regata de barcos de río, en Guntersville |
| **October**<br>South Alabama State Fair<br>National Shrimp Festival<br>in Gulf Shores | Octubre<br>Feria del sur del estado de Alabama<br>Festival nacional del camarón, en Gulf Shores |
| **November**<br>Veterans Day Parade<br>in Birmingham<br>Annual Thanksgiving Day Pow Wow<br>in Atmore | Noviembre<br>Desfile del Día de los Veteranos,<br>en Birmingham<br>Pow Wow anual del Día de Acción<br>de Gracias, en Atmore |
| **December**<br>Magic Christmas Lights Show in<br>Bellingrath Gardens | Diciembre<br>Espectáculo de las luces mágicas de<br>Navidad en Bellingrath Gardens |

# Alabama Facts/Datos sobre Alabama

**Population**
4.5 million

**Población**
4.5 millones

**Capital**
Montgomery

**Capital**
Montgomery

**State Motto**
We Dare to Defend
our Rights

**Lema del estado**
Nos atrevemos a defender
nuestros derechos

**State Flower**
Camellia

**Flor del estado**
Camelia

**State Bird**
Yellowhammer

**Ave del estado**
Emberizo

**State Nickname**
The Heart of Dixie

**Mote del estado**
El Corazón del Dixie

**State Tree**
Southern Longleaf Pine

**Árbol del estado**
Piñonero (Pino de hoja larga)

**State Song**
"Alabama"

**Canción del estado**
"Alabama"

**State Gemstone**
Star blue quartz

**Piedra preciosa**
Cuarzo estrellado azul

# Famous Alabamians/Alabamienses famosos

**Rosa Parks**
*(1913– )*

Civil rights leader
Líder de los derechos civiles

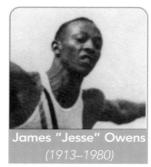
**James "Jesse" Owens**
*(1913–1980)*

Olympic gold medalist
Campeón olímpico

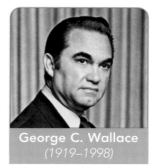
**George C. Wallace**
*(1919–1998)*

Alabama governor
Gobernador de Alabama

**Nat "King" Cole**
*(1919–1965)*

Entertainer
Músico y cantante

**Nelle Harper Lee**
*(1926– )*

Author
Autora

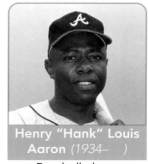
**Henry "Hank" Louis Aaron** *(1934– )*

Baseball player
Jugador de béisbol

## Words to Know/Palabras que debes saber

**border**
frontera

**march**
marcha

**mound**
montículo

**waterfall**
cascada

## Here are more books to read about Alabama:
## Otros libros que puedes leer sobre Alabama:

**In English/En inglés:**

*Alabama*
America the Beautiful Series
By Davis, Lucile
Children's Press, 1999

*Alabama*
Rookie Read
By Leber, Holli
World Almanac Library, 2004

Words in English: 284

Palabras en español: 306

# Index

# Índice